To Judy—MJ
To all living beings in all directions—TS

First published in North America in 2000 by

Loyola Press

3441 North Ashland Avenue
Chicago, Illinois 60657

Original edition published in English under the title
Classic Bible Verses for Children by Lion Publishing plc,
Oxford, England
Copyright © Lion Publishing plc 1999

Text selected and introduced by Mary Joslin
Illustrations copyright © 1999 Tom Saeker

Acknowledgments
Scripture selections marked NAB are from the New
American Bible, copyright © 1991, 1986, 1970 by the
Confraternity of Christian Doctrine, Washington, D.C.,
and are used by license of copyright owner. All rights
reserved.

Scripture selections marked NJB are from the New
Jerusalem Bible © 1993 and 1989 by Darton, Longman &
Todd, Ltd., and Doubleday, a division of Bantam
Doubleday Dell, Inc. Reprinted by permission.

Scripture selections marked NRSV are from the New
Revised Standard Version Bible: Catholic Edition copyright
© 1993 and 1989 by the Division of Christian Education
of the National Council of the Churches of Christ in the
U.S.A. Used by permission. All rights reserved.

ISBN 0-8294-1487-8

Printed and bound in Singapore
00 01 02 03 04 / 10 9 8 7 6 5 4 3 2 1

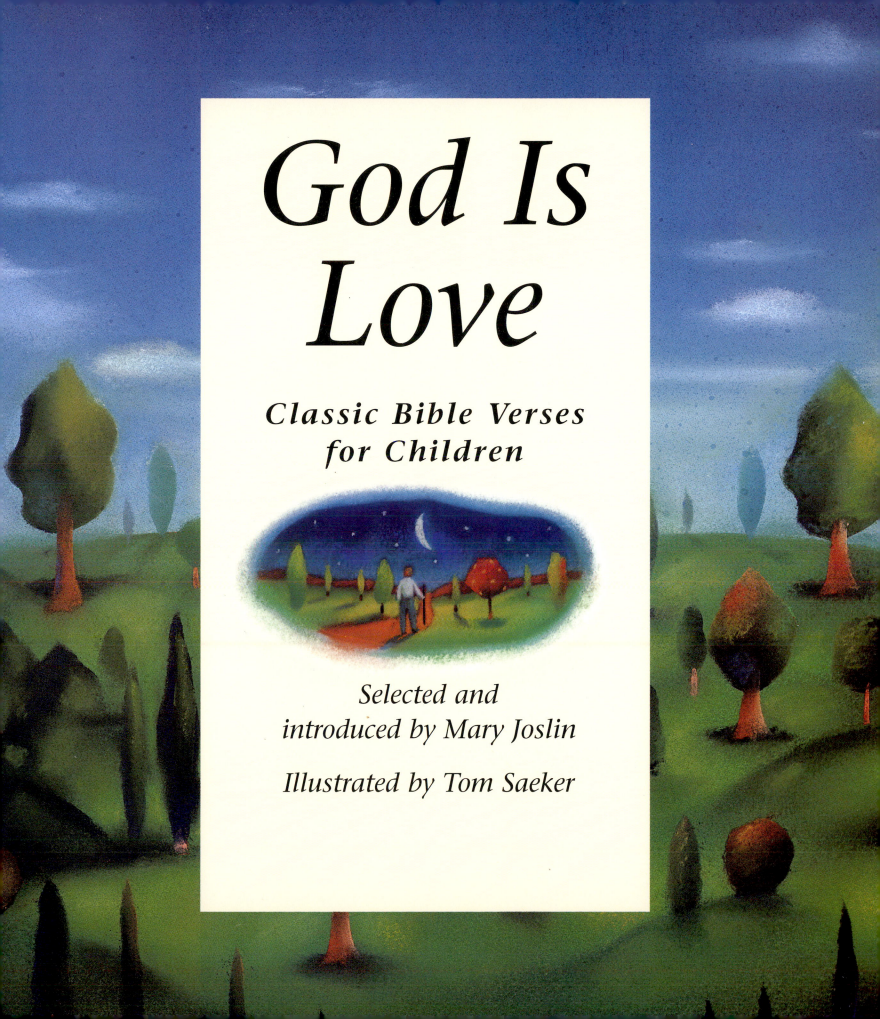

God Is Love

Classic Bible Verses for Children

Selected and
introduced by Mary Joslin

Illustrated by Tom Saeker

The Making of the World

*This ancient story is from the Bible. It tells of God's
creating a good and lovely world.*

*I*n the beginning, when God created the
heavens and the earth, the earth was a formless
wasteland, and darkness covered the abyss,
while a mighty wind swept over the waters.

Then God said, "Let there be light," and there
was light. God saw how good the light was. God
then separated the light from the darkness. God
called the light "day," and the darkness he called
"night." Thus evening came, and morning followed—the first day.

Then God said, "Let there be a dome in the middle of the waters,
to separate one body of water from the other." And so it happened:
God made the dome, and it separated the water above the dome
from the water below it. God called the dome, "the sky." Evening
came, and morning followed—the second day.

Then God said, "Let the water under the sky be gathered into a
single basin, so that the dry land may appear." And so it happened:
God called the dry land "the earth," and the basin of the water he
called "the sea." God saw how good it was. Then God said, "Let the
earth bring forth vegetation: every kind of plant that bears seed and
every kind of fruit tree on earth that bears fruit with its seed in it."
And so it happened: the earth brought forth every kind of plant that
bears seed and every kind of fruit tree on earth that bears fruit with
its seed in it. God saw how good it was. Evening came, and morning
followed—the third day.

Then God said, "Let there be lights in the dome of the sky, to separate day from night. Let them mark the fixed times, the days and years, and serve as luminaries in the dome of the sky, to shed light upon the earth." And so it happened: God made the two great lights, the greater one to govern the day, and the lesser one to govern the night; and he made the stars. God set them in the dome of the sky, to shed light upon the earth, to govern the day and the night, and to separate the light from the darkness. God saw how good it was. Evening came and morning followed—the fourth day.

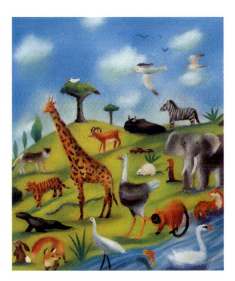

Then God said, "Let the water teem with an abundance of living creatures, and on earth let birds fly beneath the dome of the sky." And so it happened: God created the great sea monsters and all kinds of swimming creatures with which the water teems, and all kinds of winged birds. God saw how good it was, and God blessed them, saying, "Be fertile, multiply, and fill the water of the seas; and let the birds multiply on the earth." Evening came and morning followed—the fifth day.

Then God said, "Let the earth bring forth all kinds of living creatures: cattle, creeping things, and wild animals of all kinds." And so it happened: God made all kinds of wild animals, all kinds of cattle, and all kinds of creeping things of the earth. God saw how good it was.

Then God said: "Let us make man in our image, after our likeness. Let them have dominion over the fish of the sea, the birds of the air, and the cattle, and over all the wild animals and all the creatures that crawl on the ground."

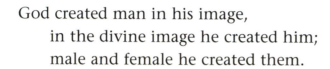

God created man in his image,
in the divine image he created him;
male and female he created them.

God blessed them, saying: "Be fertile and multiply; fill the earth and subdue it. Have dominion over the fish of the sea, the birds of the air, and all the living things that move upon the earth." God also said: "See, I give you every seed-bearing plant all over the earth and every tree that has seed-bearing fruit on it to be your food; and to all the animals of the land, all the birds of the air, and all the living creatures that crawl on the ground, I give all the green plants for food." And so it happened. God looked at everything he had made, and he found it very good. Evening came, and morning followed—the sixth day.

Thus the heavens and the earth and all their array were completed. Since on the seventh day God was finished the work he had been doing, he rested on the seventh day from all the work he had undertaken. So God blessed the seventh day and made it holy, because on it he rested from all the work he had done in creation.

Genesis 1:1–2:3, NAB

A Straight Path

Words of advice from thousands of years ago.
They tell people how to live as God wants them to.

*T*rust in the LORD with all your heart,
    on your own intelligence rely not;
In all your ways be mindful of him,
    and he will make straight your paths.

Be not wise in your own eyes,
    fear the LORD and turn away from evil. . . .

Refuse no one the good on which he has a claim
    when it is in your power to do it for him.
Say not to your neighbor, "Go, and come again,
    tomorrow I will give," when you can give at once.

Plot no evil against your neighbor,
    against him who lives at peace with you.
Quarrel not with a man without cause,
    with one who has done you no harm.
Envy not the lawless man
    and choose none of his ways. . . .

The path of the wicked enter not,
    walk not on the way of evil men;
Shun it, cross it not,
    turn aside from it, and pass on.

The way of the wicked is like darkness;
    they know not on what they stumble.
But the path of the just is like shining light,
    that grows in brilliance till perfect day.

With closest custody, guard your heart,
    for in it are the sources of life.
Put away from you dishonest talk,
    deceitful speech put far from you.
Let your eyes look straight ahead
    and your glance be directly forward.
Survey the path for your feet,
    and let all your ways be sure.
Turn neither to right nor to left,
    keep your foot far from evil.

Proverbs 3:5–7, 27–31; 4:14–15, 19–18, 23–27, NAB

Flowers in the Wilderness

*Someone dreamed long ago that God will someday
fix everything that has gone wrong in the world, and
a path will be opened to a place of joy and happiness. People
will find their way to a city they can call home—their Jerusalem.*

♥

 *T*he wilderness and the dry land shall be glad,
    the desert shall rejoice and blossom. . . .
They shall see the glory of the Lord,
    the majesty of our God.

Strengthen the weak hands,
    and make firm the feeble knees.
Say to those who are of a fearful heart,
    "Be strong, do not fear!
Here is your God.
    He will come with vengeance,
with terrible recompense.
    He will come and save you."

Then the eyes of the blind shall be opened,
    and the ears of the deaf unstopped;
then the lame shall leap like a deer,
    and the tongue of the speechless sing for joy.
For waters shall break forth in the wilderness,
    and streams in the desert;
the burning sand shall become a pool,
    and the thirsty ground springs of water;
the haunt of jackals shall become a swamp,
    the grass shall become reeds and rushes.

A highway shall be there,
    and it shall be called the Holy Way;
the unclean shall not travel on it,
    but it shall be for God's people;
    no traveler, not even fools, shall go astray.
No lion shall be there,
    nor shall any ravenous beast come up on it;
they shall not be found there,
    but the redeemed shall walk there.
And the ransomed of the LORD shall return,
    and come to Zion with singing;
everlasting joy shall be upon their heads;
    they shall obtain joy and gladness,
    and sorrow and sighing shall flee away.

Isaiah 35:1–10, NRSV

Fear No Evil

Think of a shepherd taking care of his sheep.
God is like a shepherd to people.
He gives them all they need.

*T*he LORD is my shepherd, I shall not want.
    He makes me lie down in green pastures;
he leads me beside still waters;
    he restores my soul.
He leads me in right paths
    for his name's sake.

Even though I walk through the darkest valley,
    I fear no evil;
for you are with me;
    your rod and your staff—
    they comfort me.

You prepare a table before me
    in the presence of my enemies;
you anoint my head with oil;
    my cup overflows.
Surely goodness and mercy shall follow me
    all the days of my life,
and I shall dwell in the house of the LORD
    my whole life long.

Psalm 23, NRSV

The Lost Sheep

Two thousand years ago, a baby called Jesus was born.
Some believed that he was God and had come in person to bring
love to the world. Jesus told this story:

Which one of you with a hundred sheep, if he lost one, would fail to leave the ninety-nine in the desert and go after the missing one till he found it? And when he found it, would he not joyfully take it on his shoulders and then, when he got home, call together his friends and neighbors, saying to them, 'Rejoice with me, I have found my sheep that was lost.' In the same way, I tell you, there will be more rejoicing in heaven over one sinner repenting than over ninety-nine upright people who have no need of repentance."

Luke 15:4–7, NJB

Jesus also said:

I am the good shepherd. I know my own and my own know me, just as the Father knows me and I know the Father. And I lay down my life for the sheep."

John 10:14–15, NRSV

God's Blessing

What does it mean to be blessed? It means that God does great and good things to help you. And whom does God help? This is what Jesus said:

♥

Blessed are the poor in spirit,
 for theirs is the kingdom of heaven.
Blessed are they who mourn,
 for they will be comforted.
Blessed are the meek,
 for they will inherit the land.
Blessed are they who hunger and thirst for righteousness,
 for they will be satisfied.
Blessed are the merciful,
 for they will be shown mercy.
Blessed are the clean of heart,
 for they will see God.
Blessed are the peacemakers,
 for they will be called children of God.
Blessed are they who are persecuted for the sake of righteousness,
 for theirs is the kingdom of heaven."

Matthew 5:3–10, NAB

*B*lessed are you when people revile you and persecute you and utter all kinds of evil against you falsely on my account. Rejoice and be glad, for your reward is great in heaven, for in the same way they persecuted the prophets who were before you."

Matthew 5:11–12, NRSV

Everyday Wisdom

*Jesus showed people how to live as
friends of God. Here are some of his words:*

You have heard that it was said, 'You shall love your neighbor
and hate your enemy.' But I say to you, Love your enemies and
pray for those who persecute you, so that you may be children
of your Father in heaven; for he makes his sun rise on the evil
and on the good, and sends rain on the righteous and on the
unrighteous. For if you love those who love you, what reward
do you have?. . . Be perfect, therefore, as your heavenly Father
is perfect."

Matthew 5:43–48, NRSV

So when you give alms, do not have it trumpeted before you;
this is what the hypocrites do in the synagogues and in the
streets to win human admiration. In truth I tell you, they have
had their reward. But when you give alms, your left hand must
not know what your right is doing; your almsgiving must be
secret, and your Father who sees all that is done in secret will
reward you."

Matthew 6:2–4, NJB

*D*o not store up treasures for yourselves on earth, where moth and woodworm destroy them and thieves can break in and steal. But store up treasures for yourselves in heaven, where neither moth nor woodworm destroys them and thieves cannot break in and steal. For wherever your treasure is, there will your heart be too."

Matthew 6:19–21, NJB

*D*o not judge, and you will not be judged; because the judgments you give are the judgments you will get, and the standard you use will be the standard used for you."

Matthew 7:1–2, NJB

Prayer

*Jesus said that people can talk to God in prayer
as they might talk to a parent who loves them.*

♥

*A*nd whenever you pray, do not be like the
hypocrites; for they love to stand and pray in the
synagogues and at the street corners, so that they
may be seen by others. Truly I tell you, they have
received their reward. But whenever you pray, go
into your room and shut the door and pray to your
Father who is in secret; and your Father who sees in secret
will reward you.

"When you are praying, do not heap up empty phrases as the
Gentiles do; for they think that they will be heard because of
their many words. Do not be like them, for your Father knows
what you need before you ask him.

"Pray then in this way:

Our Father in heaven,
    hallowed be your name.
    Your kingdom come.
    Your will be done,
        on earth as it is in heaven.
    Give us this day our daily bread.
    And forgive us our debts,
        as we also have forgiven our debtors.
    And do not bring us to the time of trial,
        but rescue us from the evil one.
For if you forgive others their trespasses, your heavenly
Father will also forgive you; but if you do not forgive others,
neither will your Father forgive your trespasses."

Matthew 6:5–15, NRSV

Love One Another

One day a teacher of the Law tried to trap Jesus.
He asked Jesus, "Master, what must I do
to inherit eternal life?"

He said to him, "What is written in the Law? What is your reading of it?" He replied, "You must love the Lord your God with all your heart, with all your soul, with all your strength, and with all your mind, and your neighbor as yourself." Jesus said to him, "You have answered right, do this and life is yours."

But the man was anxious to justify himself and said to Jesus, "And who is my neighbor?" In answer Jesus said, "A man was once on his way down from Jerusalem to Jericho and fell into the hands of bandits; they stripped him, beat him, and then made off, leaving him half dead. Now a priest happened to be traveling down the same road, but when he saw the man, he passed by on the other side. In the same way a Levite who came to the place saw him, and passed by on the other side. But a Samaritan traveler who came on

him was moved with compassion when he saw him. He went up to him and bandaged his wounds, pouring oil and wine on them. He then lifted him onto his own mount and took him to an inn and looked after him. Next day, he took out two denarii and handed them to the innkeeper and said, 'Look after him, and on my way back I will make good any extra expense you have.' Which of these three, do you think, proved himself a neighbor to the man who fell into the bandits' hands?" He replied, "The one who showed pity toward him." Jesus said to him, "Go and do the same yourself."

Luke 10:26–37, NJB

A New Commandment

Jesus said this to his close friends:

I give you a new commandment, that you love one another. Just as I have loved you, you also should love one another."

John 13:34, NRSV

God Is Love

One of Jesus' followers was named John.
When Jesus left this world and went to God in heaven,
John spread the message that Jesus had taught.

For this is the message you have heard from the beginning: we should love one another.

1 John 3:11, NAB

If someone who has worldly means sees a brother in need and refuses him compassion, how can the love of God remain in him? Children, let us love not in word or speech but in deed and truth.

1 John 3:17–18, NAB

My dear friends,
let us love one another,
since love is from God
and everyone who loves
      is a child of God and knows God.
Whoever fails to love does not know God,
because God is love.
This is the revelation
      of God's love for us,
that God sent his only Son into the world
that we might have life through him.

1 John 4:7–9, NJB

We love because he first loved us. Those who
say, "I love God," and hate their brothers or sisters,
are liars; for those who do not love a brother or
sister whom they have seen, cannot love God
whom they have not seen. The commandment we
have from him is this: those who love God must
love their brothers and sisters also.

1 John 4:19–21, NRSV

The Rich, the Poor

A follower of Jesus, named James,
told people they must be fair in showing love to others.

*F*or if a man with gold rings on his fingers and in fine clothes comes into your assembly, and a poor person in shabby clothes also comes in, and you pay attention to the one wearing the fine clothes and say, "Sit here, please," while you say to the poor one, "Stand there," or "Sit at my feet," have you not made distinctions among yourselves and become judges with evil designs?

Listen, my beloved brothers. Did not God choose those who are poor in the world to be rich in faith and heirs of the kingdom that he promised to those who love him? But you dishonored the poor person. Are not the rich oppressing you? And do they themselves not haul you off to court? Is it not they who blaspheme the noble name that was invoked over you? However, if you fulfill the royal law according to the scripture, "You shall love your neighbor as yourself," you are doing well.

James 2:2–8, NAB

Love Forever

Only love is forever, said a follower of Jesus named Paul.

*I*f I speak in the tongues of mortals and of angels, but do not have love, I am a noisy gong or a clanging cymbal. And if I have prophetic powers, and understand all mysteries and all knowledge, and if I have all faith, so as to remove mountains, but do not have love, I am nothing. If I give away all my possessions, and if I hand over my body so that I may boast, but do not have love, I gain nothing.

Love is patient; love is kind; love is not envious or boastful or arrogant or rude. It does not insist on its own way; it is not irritable or resentful; it does not rejoice in wrongdoing, but rejoices in the truth. It bears all things, believes all things, hopes all things, endures all things.

Love never ends. But as for prophecies, they will come to an end;
as for tongues, they will cease; as for knowledge, it will come to an
end. For we know only in part, and we prophesy only in part; but
when the complete comes, the partial will come to an end. When I
was a child, I spoke like a child, I thought like a child, I reasoned
like a child; when I became an adult, I put an end to childish ways.
For now we see in a mirror, dimly, but then we will see face to face.
Now I know only in part; then I will know fully, even as I have been
fully known. And now faith, hope, and love abide, these three; and
the greatest of these is love.

1 Corinthians 13:1–13, NRSV